Margaret Mahy

LEAF MAGIC

pictures by
Jenny Williams

Parents' Magazine Press

New York

First published by J. M. Dent & Sons Ltd, London
Text copyright © Margaret Mahy 1976
Illustrations copyright © J. M. Dent & Sons Ltd 1976
All rights reserved
Printed in the United States of America 1977

Library of Congress Cataloging in Publication Data

Mahy, Margaret.
  Leaf magic.
  SUMMARY: Michael desperately wants a dog but all
he gets is a big orange leaf that follows him everywhere.
    1. [Dogs—Fiction. 2. Magic—Fiction]
I. Williams, Jenny, 1939- II. Title.
PZ7.M2773Le3 [E] 76-3538
ISBN 0-8193-0889-7 ISBN 0-8193-0890-0 lib. bdg.

10 9 8 7 6 5 4 3 2 1

When Michael ran home from school, he heard the wind at his heels rustling like a dog in the grass. As he ran a thought came into his mind.

"I wish I had a dog. Running would be more fun with a dog."

The way home wound through a spinney of trees. It was autumn and the trees were like bonfires, burning arrows and fountains of gold. But Michael ran past without even seeing them.

"I wish I had a dog," he said aloud in time to his running.

The trees heard him and rustled to each other.

"A dog with a whisking tail," Michael added.

The wind ran past him. Michael tried to whistle to it, but the wind is nobody's dog and goes only where it wants to. It threw a handful of bright and stolen leaves all over Michael and went off leaping among the trees. Michael thought for a moment that he could see its tail whisking in the grass. He brushed the leaves off his shoulder.

"An orange sort of dog with a whisking tail,"
Michael went on, making up a dog out of autumn
and out of the wind.

The trees rustled again as he left them behind
and came out onto the road. Patter, patter,
patter. Something was following him.

"It's my dog," Michael thought, but he did not
turn around, in case it wasn't.

Patter, patter, patter. . . . At last Michael just *had* to look over his shoulder. A big orange leaf was following him – too big to come from any tree that Michael knew. When he stopped, the leaf stopped too. He went on again. Patter, patter, patter went the leaf, following him.

Some men working on the roadside laughed to see a leaf following a boy. Michael grew angry with the leaf and ran faster to get away from it. The faster he ran, the faster the leaf followed him, tossing and tumbling like a clown, head over heels in the stones along the roadside.

No matter how he tacked and dodged on the way
home, he could not lose the leaf. He crawled
through a hedge – but the leaf flew over it, light
and rustling.

He jumped over a creek and the leaf jumped after
him. What was worse, it jumped better than he
did.

He was glad to get home
and shut the door behind him.
The leaf could not get in.

Later that evening his mother went
to close the curtains. She laughed and
said, "There's such a big autumn leaf out here
on the window sill, and it's fluttering up and
down like a moth trying to get at the light.
It looks as if it's alive."
"Don't let it in," said Michael quickly.
"I think it's something horrible
pretending to look like
a leaf."

He was glad when his mother pulled the
curtains, but that night when he lay in bed,
something rustled and sighed on his own
window sill, and he knew it was the leaf.

Next day it followed him to school. As he sat at his lessons, he saw it dancing like a flame out in the playground, waiting for him. When he went out to play, it bounced at his heels. Michael made up his mind to trap the leaf. He chased after it, but it wouldn't let itself be caught. It crouched and then flittered away. It teased him and tricked him. Michael felt that leaf was enjoying itself thoroughly. Everybody laughed but Michael.

At last he decided he must be under some witch's spell.

"I'll have to go and ask Fish and Chips about it," he thought. "He'll know what to do."

Fish and Chips was an old whiskery man who lived in a cottage by the sea. He had built it himself. The walls were made of driftwood and fish bones and it was thatched with seaweed. Fish and Chips was not only whiskery but wise as well. He was almost a wizard really.

After school, instead of going home by the trees, Michael ran down onto the beach. He left a trail of footmarks behind him in the soft sand, and the leaf skipped happily in and out of them. Once it rushed down to the sea to taste the salt water. Once it sailed up to where the sand ended and the grass began, but all the time it was really following Michael closely.

Fish and Chips was sitting at the door of his house. Michael ran right up to him, but the leaf stayed a short distance away, playing by itself and watching them.

"Ah," said Fish and Chips, "I see you are being haunted. Do you want me to help you?"

"Yes please," said Michael. "That leaf has been following me since yesterday."

"It must like you," Fish and Chips remarked.

"But I don't want it," Michael said. "Can you catch it?"

"Oh yes, I think so," Fish and Chips replied. "It seems friendly and full of curiosity. Let us hide behind the door and see if it comes after us."

They hid behind the door
with the brooms, rubber boots,
raincoats and milk bottles all
belonging to Fish and Chips.
Through a crack in the door
Michael could see the leaf coming
closer and closer. It hesitated on the
threshold of the cabin and
then came in.

"Now!" said Fish and Chips, and Michael slammed the door shut while Fish and Chips jumped out and caught the leaf. Michael saw it twisting for a moment in his brown hands, as if he was holding a little fire. Then Fish and Chips opened a big box and dropped the leaf in. The lid slammed down. The big orange leaf was shut up alone in the dark.

"It won't trouble you again," Fish and Chips
told him.

"Thank you very much," Michael said politely.
"How much do I owe you?"

"Whistle a sea chanty for me," Fish and Chips
replied. "Whistle it into this bottle and I'll be able
to use it again sometime."

So Michael whistled "What Shall We Do with the Drunken Sailor" into the bottle. Then Fish and Chips corked it up quickly before the tune had time to get out. As Michael left, he was writing a label for it.

Michael set out for home slowly across the beach. All the time he was listening for the rustling of the leaf behind him. He kept looking back over his shoulder. Half way across the beach he stopped. The beach looked empty without that bright leaf tossing behind him.

He thought of it shut up in that dark box in the
seaweed-and-fishbones cabin. How it would hate
being boxed up. Suddenly he found he was missing
the leaf. Michael took one more step and then
he turned round and went back to Fish and
Chips' cabin.

Fish and Chips
was putting the bottle
up on a high shelf.

"What, more leaves already?"
he asked.

"Well, not exactly," Michael said
in a small voice. "I just decided
I wanted the old one back
after all."

"Oh well," said Fish and Chips.
"Often people do want them back,
but they don't often get them back,
not quite the same. They change,
you know."

"Change?" asked Michael.

"Like that," said Fish and Chips.

Fish and Chips opened his box. Out jumped a big orange dog with a whisking tail.

The dog put its paw on Michael's chest and licked his face.

"My dog," Michael cried. "It's my dog!"

He took its paw in his hands and they danced until the fishbones rattled.

"Thank you, thank you," Michael called to Fish and Chips.

"Don't thank me," Fish and Chips said. "You did it all by coming back for your leaf. That's the way with magic. But just get out of my cabin now, before you shake the fishbones down."

Michael leaped out laughing, and raced off along the beach. The dog came bounding after him and they set out for home. As they ran under the trees, leaves fell over them like a shower of gold. The wind tried to join in the chase, but Michael and his dog were too fast for it.

Trying to pretend it did not care, the wind made
itself a bright scarf out of the fallen leaves and
watched Michael and his autumn dog speed up
the road, burrow through a hedge, jump the creek
and come home at last. Laughing to itself, the wind
swept into a shining bush and sat there rustling
like a salamander in the heart of a fire.

MARGARET MAHY *grew up in a little town* "*where the river met the sea, close under hills covered with dense New Zealand bush.*" *And when she was very young, Margaret wrote stories for her school magazine and the children's page of a local newspaper. She had a brief career in nursing but then returned to college and library school. Today she works as a librarian and continues to write her fanciful stories for children* — *in* "*a lovely new house by the sea*" *where she lives with her two daughters. She has twice won the Esther Glen Award of the New Zealand Library Association, and a number of her books have been published in the United States, including* . The Witch in the Cherry Tree *and* Ultra-Violet Catastrophe! *by Parents' Magazine Press.*

JENNY WILLIAMS *began drawing when she was a little girl in England shortly after World War II, but drawing paper was hard to get. Often she tore the fly leaves out of books and used those.* "*After all, I thought they were spare, so I felt quite justified in putting them to good use.*" *Later she attended Wimbledon Art School and London University. She designed jackets for adult books and worked in advertising and fashion illustration before she began illustrating books for children. She has written some of her own picture books and illustrated several by Margaret Mahy. Jenny Williams and her husband live in Wales.*